Gargoyle (**GAHR**-goil): A waterspout in
the form of a grotesque human or animal
figure projecting from the roof or eaves
of a building.

For Glenn, who admires gargoyles
—E.B.
For Dorothy Briley
—D.W.

Clarion Books
a Houghton Mifflin Company imprint
215 Park Avenue South, New York, NY 10003
Text copyright © 1994 by Eve Bunting
Illustrations copyright © 1994 by David Wiesner
Illustrations executed in pastel on four-ply Strathmore drawing paper
Text is 18-point Lucian
Book design and typography by Carol Goldenberg
Printed in duotone by The Stinehour Press

Library of Congress Cataloging-in-Publication Data
Bunting, Eve, 1928–
Night of the gargoyles / by Eve Bunting ; illustrated by David Wiesner.
p. cm.
Summary: In the middle of the night, the gargoyles that adorn the walls of an art museum
come to life and frighten the night watchman.
ISBN 0-395-66553-1
[1. Gargoyles—Fiction. 2. Horror stories.] I. Wiesner, David,
ill. II. Title.
PZ7.B91527Nh 1994
[E]—dc20   93-8160
CIP AC

HOR 10 9 8 7 6 5 4 3 2 1

NIGHT OF THE GARGOYLES

by Eve Bunting
Illustrated by David Wiesner

CLARION BOOKS ❧ NEW YORK

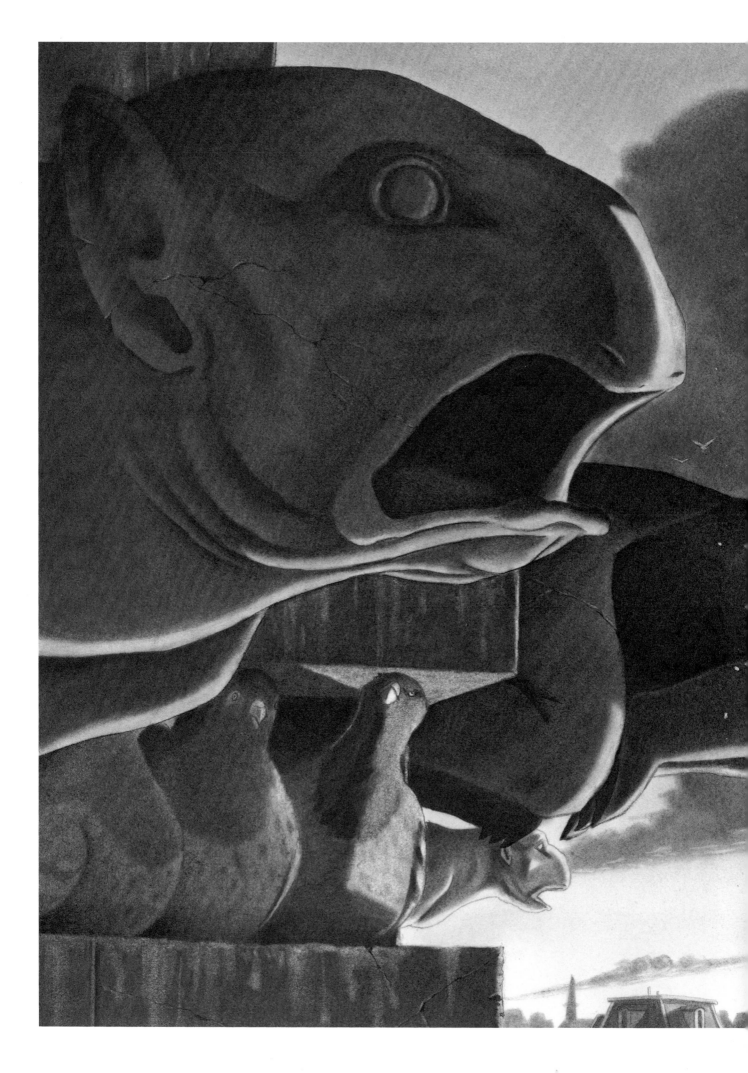

The gargoyles squat
high on corners
staring into space,
their empty eyes unblinking

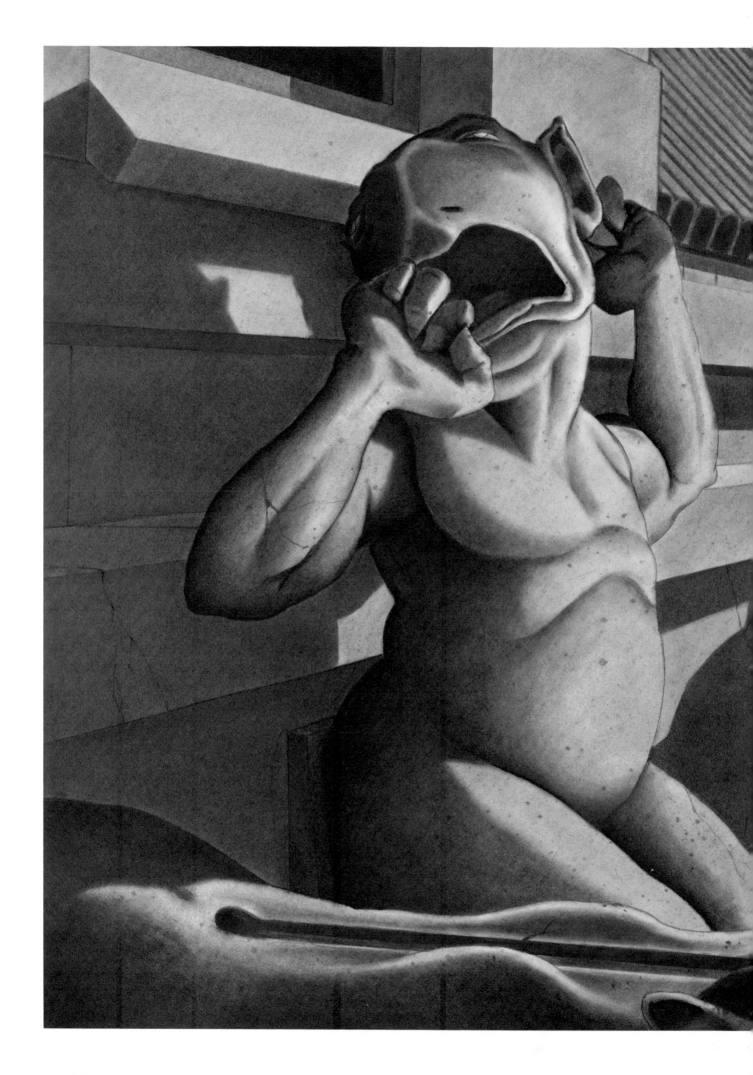

till night comes.

Then there is movement
in the shadowy corners
as the gargoyles creep
on stubs of feet
along the high ledges
and peer,
nearsighted,
into rooms where mummies lie
in boxes, long and thin
as coffins, ribboned round
with painted boats and figures
dark as night.

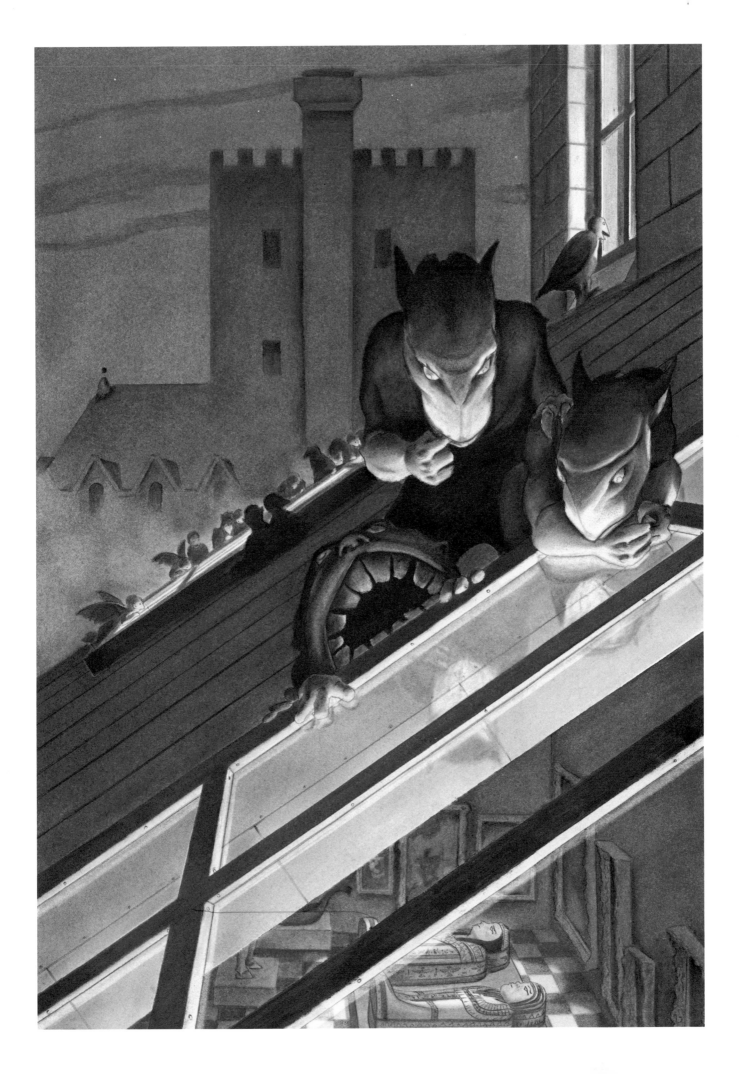

And gargoyle-creep again
to gape at suits of armor,
shining, stiff,
the helmets hinged on eyes
as bloodless as their own.

Or, tired of viewing,
fly, if they have gargoyle wings,
straight up to lick the stars
with long, stone tongues
green-pickled at the edges.
Or land in sleeping trees
to swing on branches, da-de-da,
and feel the air move cool
against their pockmarked stone.

Then down they swoop
to where a fountain splashes dark,
the water spitting from a cherub's mouth.
They gargoyle-hunch around the rim
and gargoyle-grunt
with friends from other corners
who have come for company.

They grunt of what they've seen
and where they've been.
How hot the corners
when the sun is high,
especially the ones beside the clock.
How noisy, too.

They grump of summer passing
and the rain
that pours in torrents through
their gaping lips
and chokes their throats
with autumn's leaves.

And then those birds
that come to rudely perch
and leave behind
their mottled stains.

They lap the water
with their mossy tongues,
split-splat each other with their claws
and boom those gargoyle laughs
that rumble thick
because there is no space
inside their solid stone
for laughs to somersault.

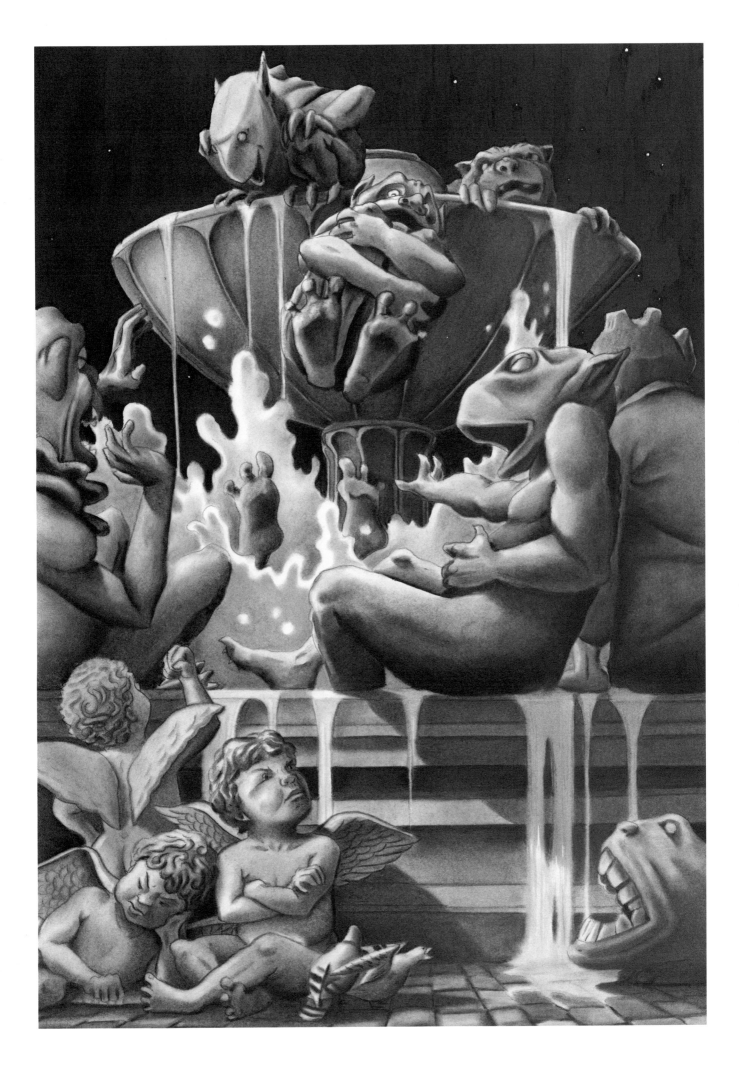

A watchman hurries by
and checks the sky
for thunder.
He's seen the gargoyles
huddle there before,
and once he told
the man behind the frosted door
and heard him snort his disbelief.
"Gargoyles, indeed!
You're seeing things."

So now he checks the sky
to hide his fear.

The gargoyles rasp their wings
and put their thumbs behind
their crumbling ears
to show their scorn.

They have no love of humans
who have made them so
and set them high
on ledges
where dark pigeons go.
They stomp their feet
and rumble-laugh
to see the watchman close his eyes
and turn away.

"Awk!" the gargoyles scream,
and "Awk!" again,
and spread their lips
in mischief smiles.

The watchman hunches down
and hurries on.

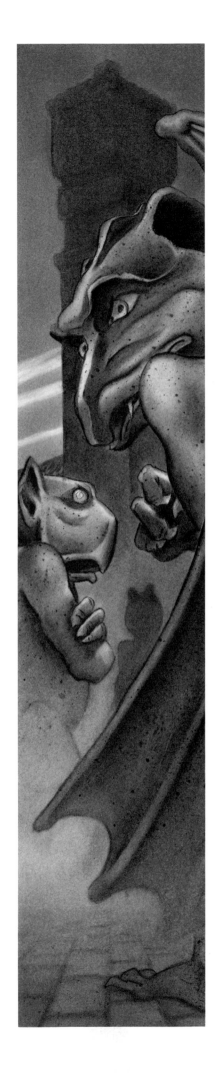

It's almost morning now
and so the gargoyles fly,
or wingless crawl
up walls
as spiders do.
They take their corners
quietly
and stare
and stare,
their empty eyes unblinking

till night comes.

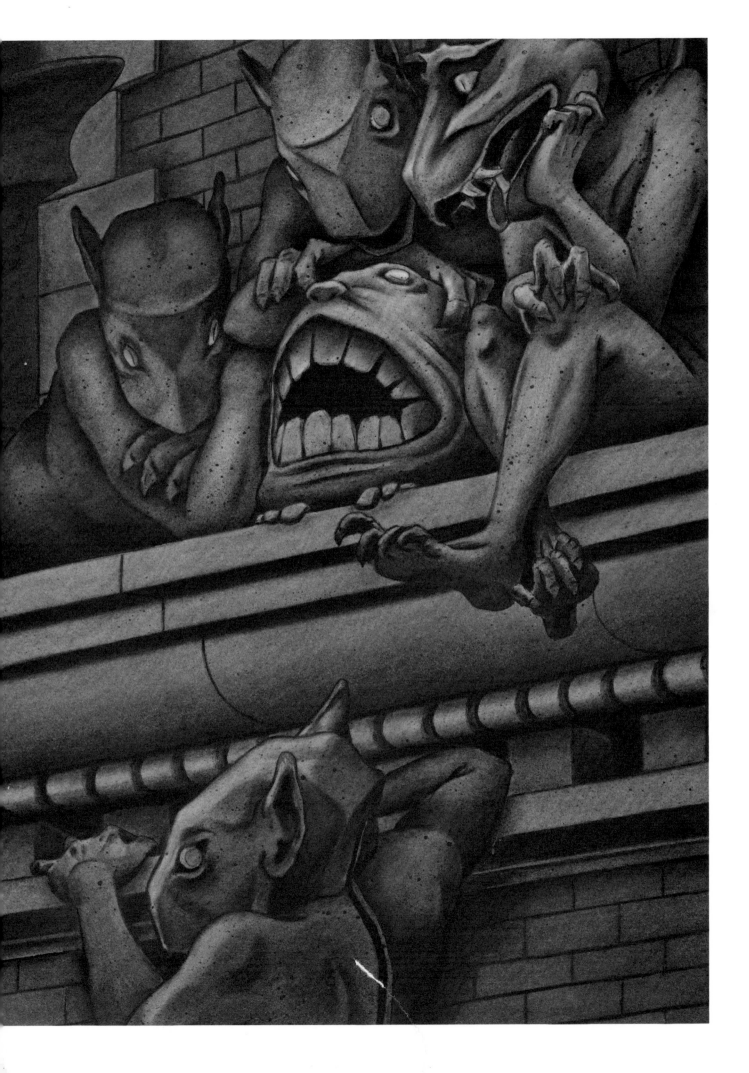